A Covid
Christmas Carol

Copyright

First published 2020 by Junco Books,
Brooklyn, NY
juncobooks.com

ISBN: 978-1-7347691-7-3 (Paperback)

A Covid Christmas Carol

By

Evan Sykes

Preface

I HAVE endeavoured in this Ghostly little holiday book, to put to rest certain ideas of what might be considered a "friendly host"—one Gasper the friendly host, in particular—and in doing so I have hoped to make the reader smile rather than scowl, grimace, sulk, bellow, scream or weep and cry as we have too often done in this unpleasantly uneventful year of 2020.

Evan Sykes
December, 2020

Stave I

A Beginning and an End

WE MUST START at the beginning and we must lose no time at all. The season of goodwill is upon us, and although the days before the 25th might seem to drag interminably to those who posted early their letters to a certain Mr. Claus—precise address unknown, but proximal to what remains of the North Pole—for the rest of us these days of merriment, goodwill, gluttony and drink will fly by, as a rule, at a most regrettable speed.

Too soon the decorations are coming down again! Too soon the holiday lights are put out! And far, far too soon we're trudging off to work once more on a cold and bitter morning of a newly minted year carrying with us uneasy feelings about our health, both financial and physical.

Let us lose no time then in meeting the first mover of these most singular events.

Mr. Branford Foxington-Raynor, partner in Raynor and Gasper's Dry Goods, expected no worries in the coming year 2021. He expected no worries at all. He was dead. You object that the dead may have worries like the rest of us? You contend they might even have much greater worries, scooped up from their terrestrial home where vice and folly are the norm to defend themselves before an Almighty? Very good, but here we have time only for facts.

And it was a solid fact that Foxington-Raynor was dead.

If an observer, devoid of sense, had missed this fact in the old bachelor's demeanor as he lay in his casket, it would not have mattered a jot. The coroner and the lawyers had made it perfectly clear. They'd poked around in deeds, cabinets and orifices and typed their irrefutable conclusions into the required systems in a computer network touted for its infallibility. They'd even printed out those conclusions several times as proofs in case anyone should come looking for a copy. And no one did, it must be said, except one man: Foxington-Raynor's former business parter, Anatole Gasper.

"For surety," said Gasper, deftly plucking copies of said conclusions from the hands of the professional gentlemen and checking no ambiguity remained about the following: Cause of death, heart attack; age of death, sixty-three; value at death, just over eleven million United States dollars—all of which was held in shares at Raynor and Gasper's Dry Goods, and must now be transferred to the sole remaining proprietor, Mr. Anatole Gasper.

"Heart attack at sixty-three... good..." Gasper mused, as he undertook his review. "What did the old pig expect?" He might have dodged the deadly pandemic that ravaged the planet in 2020, but Foxington-Raynor had been morbidly obese, a state of affairs he'd coupled with zero exercise, high blood pressure, and a damnable temperament that gave itself over to constant excoriations and blistering, unwarranted rage. "Of course it was his heart—or lack of it!"

This lack of a heart might have played a role in the satisfactory conclusion of the third point in question too. For, in spite of his substantial assets at death, Foxington-Raynor's passing elicited no outpouring of grief from a single earthly soul, including those Gasper most feared: souls wont to appear with the astonishing rapidity of mushrooms on rotting wood when a weak claim to a fortune was to be made.

No one bothered. No one dared. Anyone who knew Anatole Gasper, knew the paperwork would be in order and he would take possession of every penny of that tidy sum his associate had left behind.

"A job well done," Gasper concluded. There remained only the business of the funeral—generously paid for company—and to which ending we can now turn as our true beginning.

SO IT WAS THAT ONCE UPON A TIME—December twenty-third of the year 2020 to be precise—Anatole Gasper stood frozen and soaked by the graveside of his recently deceased business partner, Branford Foxington-Raynor, at the Presbyterian Cemetery on Long Island, New York, closest to the "ancestral home" of the dead.

A gale was blowing that solemn day. A fierce gale that had brought along a friend: the cold and slanting rain. Only five unwilling mourners withstood that biting weather, waiting as the pallbearers struggled to lift the coffin onto its lowering ropes. And only Gasper was neither an employee of the church, the funeral home nor the benevolent society that tasked itself with sending mourners to the funerals of lonely and detested people.

Given this bleak weather, the look on Gasper's face was not entirely appropriate for the solemn occasion at hand, but benefitted from the useful concealment of his face mask.

He was a tall man in his late fifties, pot-bellied but otherwise lean. His flesh, it seemed, had tried shrinking him into a ball at one time, but had met with strong resistance from his skeleton. Thus he was still tall but stooped, and skinny but bloated in the middle. His hair was gray, his complexion ashen, and his piercing eye all the more disturbing because it was invariably accompanied by a reticence from his mouth.

Gasper wasn't a man of particular good will towards his fellow sinners. But neither was he malicious like Foxington-Raynor had been. He simply wasn't that interested in anyone's business except his own. Still, when a fellow had struck a deal with you twenty years previously on clear and written terms that whoever "carked it first"—as Foxington-Raynor liked to say—the other would get ownership of their entire business, well, providing the business was still in existence—it was—and the value of said business was "tidy"—this was unquestionable—then you'd make the effort to stand at their graveside of an afternoon as the loser in the gamble was lowered into the ground.

It was a debt that only required payment one time, after all.

Now, the heavy rain came scudding in sideways across the tops of the surrounding headstones, penetrating the thin fabric of the ill-fitting mourning suit that Gasper had bought the previous afternoon.

Beneath him, as a huge shadow fell over the newly dug grave, the cemetery's opportunistic worms must have looked up at that enormous casket dancing and swaying on its lowering ropes and have foreseen for themselves a long season of feasting that would last until the spring, and perhaps well beyond.

With a mighty splash, the coffin found its resting place in the water and mud, and each of the pallbearers gave an uninhibited gasp of relief and set to rubbing their chaffed and frozen hands vigorously against their sides.

Gasper, however, was feeling neither physical nor sentimental pain. Behind his mask, he now appeared contented, and in his mind, he was entertaining thoughts similar to those of the worms. There was no denying this fourth quarter of 2020 was proving an exceptional success for him—a success he decided to celebrate that evening once this tedious business was over.

The pastor, a twitchy little sparrow of a man with an embryo-sized head, rapidly intoned some forgettable platitudes from behind his dripping face mask, requested all gathered join him in prayer, then, perhaps with respect for the mortal condition of those by the graveside, brought the proceedings to a quick close and signaled to all that it might now be best to get out of the wind and rain and join him in the meeting hall.

This same pastor had earlier fixed Gasper with an enquiring and beady eye in the meeting hall and asked if he wished to say a few words at the graveside after the lowering of the casket. Gasper had declined the opportunity emphatically.

"Not my thing," he'd replied. "Not my thing, at all."

And, in truth, what was there to say anyway? Foxington-Raynor had amassed a substantial fortune but no favor in the eyes of his fellow men. Any honest eulogy would need to steer clear of the deceased's philanthropy, service to humanity, humility, and general good cheer. And one could hardly tell the truth about the deceased's having been a stuck up, bad-tempered, corpulent, greedy, irascible old pig who you were glad was finally dead. Not while the gravediggers were still piling on the dirt, at least.

Once inside, the pastor had handed out towels, poured a little sherry—sherry that had been bad to begin with when the bottle was first opened at the end of the last millennium—and made his way to Gasper's side where he began to angle for cash.

"I hear the deceased was a most reliable business partner," said the pastor, his huge head tilting sideways approvingly on its sparrow-sized perch of a body.

"Oh! Most reliable," agreed Gasper, trying a sip of the sherry and eyeing the exit immediately on tasting it.

"And competent?"

"Very."

"And he left a great fortune, I believe."

"I was unaware he left anything," replied Gasper.

"But the business... the dry goods business, I mean," continued the pastor, who had done his research.

"Any money belongs to the business," was Gasper's stony reply. And no lawyer in the land would have contended the matter.

The pastor was not thwarted, however.

"I suppose, what I'm saying," he continued, rubbing his hands vigorously together as if to warm them, "is that, at this time of sad loss and of grieving, perhaps now would be a good moment to consider some provision in the service of good works."

"Good works?" The sherry alone was enough to make you choke, but that! "The company doesn't get involved in that type of thing," replied Gasper in a tone so stunningly blunt the pastor stopped his unctuous appeals for a moment. "The company will not change," Gasper added. "There will be no change in disbursements."

"I see," said the Pastor, his hands apparently sufficiently warmed now as they had dropped by his sides in a gesture that also suited a flagging enthusiasm.

"Perhaps, Mr. Gasper, in that case, you would consider a private donation to the deceased's place of—"

But he got no further.

"I'll stop you there," Gasper interrupted. "Better lives are built on hard work, not charity." And seeing his words were having the trampling effect he desired on the pastor, he dealt a swift, plain-spoken *coup de grâce*, "Charity's not my thing."

He was disburdened of his sherry glass shortly thereafter and no more words were exchanged between the two men other than a curt, "Good will to all men" barked at his back as Gasper left the meeting hall.

"Good will, and good riddance to one man in particular," was the muttered reply.

And thus the funeral business was complete. The body was disposed of, the formalities completed, the glum and ill-attended reception for a man no one liked ended, the pastor deceived in his hopes, the five-person gathering dispersed, and the doors of the fusty meeting room soon closed and locked for another day.

The miserable weather had lessened not one bit. But, dashing to his car, Gasper had a rare, warm feeling in his breast.

"Freedom!" he thought. "Free at last!"

And it was an agreeable drive he took, through that foul weather, back to Brooklyn where he had his home. Within the hour, he knew he would park close to the only restaurant he frequented. There, in spite of the pandemic, he could always find a seat and a table indoors. And there, this evening, he would celebrate, just a little, with good fare and excellent wine.

Stave II

A Heavenly Song

FOXINGTON-RAYNOR AND GASPER had never had commerce with each other outside their business, and this suited them both just fine.

On parting company each evening, Foxington-Raynor would drive home, furious at the other drivers on the road, slump in front of his television and stuff himself with trash just as he had done all day long. Gasper preferred to dine out, always at the same restaurant—Chez Robert— which was walking distance from his house. The fare here was good, it was "just right"—"correct" as the French owner, the eponymous Robert, would say—and when accompanied by a quality French wine, it met all Gasper's expectations.

Gasper liked good wines very much, and mostly he liked good wines from France though he could occasionally be persuaded to try an Italian, as long as it was both from the north and beyond the financial means of the greater part of humanity. But on special occasions, like tonight, there could be no question of anything other than a burgundy, and if you are going to celebrate—*really* celebrate—with a bottle of burgundy then it must have *Romanée* somewhere on the label.

Romanée-Conti then! And a porterhouse with creamed spinach and sautéed potatoes on the side, the ones with a hint of truffle oil.

"Excellent, Monsieur Gaspaaar!" replied the owner of the establishment with such fervor one might have thought he was about to partake of the meal himself. "And a glass of champagne, on ze house?"

"Not my thing, thank you, Robert," Gasper replied. It was an old dance between them. Champagne "on ze house" was never quality, unless it was first refused.

"Oh! But Monsieur Gaspaar! This is no Cliquot or Perrier for you! This I will open is Dom Perignon... *ze* Dom Perignon. Some little holiday bubbles, compliments of Chez Robert. Please!"

Such generosity is a hard thing to refuse. The champagne was brought and drunk. The glass was refilled once, twice. The Conti would need time to breathe, after all. But a third glass of Champagne, that was too much! It was drunk anyway. Then the porterhouse was served and the Conti came with it. The Conti had breathed, and very well too. Its lungs were full! Beside the porterhouse it now sang an exquisite duet just for Gasper while the creamed spinach and sautéd potatoes kept harmony and time in the background.

"Heaven's above!" Gasper exclaimed, loosening his collar, as the song progressed towards its coda. "Heaven's above!"

Not once in his many years of coming to Chez Robert had anyone ever seen this reliable, solitary patron so suddenly effuse and apparently uncomfortable. Robert came running to his table with panic in his eyes.

"Monsieur Gaspaar! You are okay?" he cried wringing his hands.

A terrible pause ensued. Robert stared fixedly at the table, at the man, at the table, at his hands, at the ceiling, and back at the table. The steak was gone. Three quarters of the Conti too. But Monsieur Gaspaar did not answer. He stared into space. Poor Robert! Something was wrong! A Conti had been opened, and something was wrong! Chez Robert had survived the pandemic. It had survived several months of clandestine dining. It was surviving still, on reduced capacity. But it would not survive the shame, the ignom—

"Monsieur Robert," Gasper whispered in the softened tones of a man who had just experienced a heavenly duet dancing down his throat. "Monsieur Robert," he repeated, searching again for mere words until, at last, his throat yielded up two laconic syllables, all too human but perfect for what he must express. He spoke the word slowly and with care: "Sublime."

Robert leaped, he pirouetted, he shouted for joy: Prepare ze Marquise au Chocolat! Grind ze coffee beans! Polish ze best crystal for ze house's finest Armagnac! All were soon carried to the table by a dancing Robert who apparently could hear the heavenly song making its journey through Gasper's digestive system. And each offering was impressively consumed by the quiet, satisfied individual at the table who would, in all probability, have a veritable *Ring Cycle* playing in his guts in the morning.

HAVING THUS BEGUILED THE EVENING in celebration, Gasper went home to bed. He lived in a house, not an apartment, and the house was all his. The neighborhood had once been a dingy and cheap part of Brooklyn, but had become fashionable in recent years due to its proximity to the East River. Safe to say, no ideas of fashion or desirability had informed Gasper's decision to buy the house fifteen years previously, unless saving money and avoiding other people were considered desirables.

The rain was still falling, but the wind, perhaps with a mind to cause trouble elsewhere, had abandoned the partnership and fled further up the north-east. The facade of Gasper's house stood dark, empty and solemn. He cared not in the least: it was a homecoming he was habituated to from years of bachelor life, and he was in good spirits.

Before the front door, with the rain falling through his hair and over his shoulders, Gasper spent an unwelcome moment searching his pockets over and over, looking for his door key, which he found, at length, in a corner of the first pocket he had searched in.

The next challenge was to get the key into the lock. Some force of magnetic repulsion was pushing the key in every direction except into the keyhole. Gasper took a moment's pause, lent against the door and found himself face-to-face with the head of a lion. This was no creature of flesh and blood but the vintage brass knocker Gasper had installed fifteen years previously, and which had seen very little service in the interim.

"Good evening, lion," Gasper said, failing to hold the extraordinarily steady gaze of the beast before him.

"Good evening, Gasper," the lion replied.

As might be expected, this brought Gasper to attention very quickly.

"Did you… did you… speak, lion?" he stammered.

But the door knocker had apparently said all it was going to say. Its feline face didn't so much as twitch a brass whisker.

Gasper renewed his efforts to get the key in the lock with such hurried concentration after this that he succeeded in his goal, the door flew open, and he fell forwards into his cold and dark hallway.

A moment later the lion found itself on the outside of a slammed door with the rain again falling over its unmoving brass face. The residential street was quiet but for the sound of rain falling through the barren branches of the wintering trees. And all was still—as still as that brass implacable face—except for an inexplicable shadow that stirred in a passageway to the right of Gasper's house. It had moved to a spot sheltered by an overhanging roof and fallen quite still again.

THAT ENCOUNTER HAD BEEN a strange business for sure, but like so many encounters that follow on the tails of good cheer and excellent drink, the memory of it was short and was completely extinguished by the time Gasper had turned on the lights in his house.

Hanging up his jacket now, he noticed a tickle in his throat and a sniffle in his nose.

"Must be chill from that weather earlier," he thought.

He made a hot port as remedy and retired to his front room where he slumped down on his couch to administer this medicine and catch up on the news.

But how peculiar he felt! There was a distinct dizziness too. He was a little drunk, of course, and he knew it, but not *that* drunk. Besides, Dom Perignon was, as a rule, blameless. Romanée-Conti was no less infallible than the Holy See. And that special Armagnac of Robert's was the stuff of angels. Still, dizzy he was! There was no denying it.

"That abysmal weather today must be to blame!" he sighed. But soon, he found stability in a good draft of his port, experienced a moment's gloom watching people die *en masse* wearing respirators on the television, and promptly fell into a deep and welcome slumber.

He was not, however, destined to spend the night snoring contentedly on his couch in inebriate fashion. Outside, his front door knocker was suddenly making the sound it had been created to make.

Bang! Bang! went the lion's head. Gasper grunted and turned.

Bang! Bang! went the knocker again, somewhat louder than the first time. More grunts followed a deep breath and some twitching of the head.

BANG! BANG!

"What the…!" Gasper sat bolt upright and a terrible pain shot through his head.

BANG! BANG!

"The blasted door!" he yowled. "Who the hell, at this time—" then followed a moment's confusion: wasn't there something about the door knocker—

BANG! BANG!

He stood up. His head span. He felt so weak he would have sat down again but—

BANG! BANG!

"Good God, I'm going to kill whoever this is," he thought.

He coughed. Another cough followed. This latter brought with it an ice pick to drive through Gasper's skull, which was promptly done.

BANG! BANG!

Gasper threw open his front door ready to strangle whoever it might be.

It was a youth, male, early twenties perhaps, and, beneath the falling rain, in the gloomy winter night, he looked as dejected a creature as Gasper had ever seen.

Stave III

A Visitor

"Mr. Gasper?" the wretched-looking youth inquired.

"What do you want?" was the furious reply.

Perhaps the youth hadn't expected such hostility. He tried for universal goodwill:

"Merry Christmas and Happy Holidays!" he said, chirpily.

"Merry what? Bug off! You've no business banging on doors at this time of night with your Merry Christmases."

"I'm sorry. I know you don't know me, Mr. Gasper, but—" he said.

"So much the better for me," Gasper interrupted. A heat was rising under his collar that contrasted strangely with the shivers in his spine. "Beat it!" he shouted, and these words of good cheer delivered, he was seized by a paroxysm of wheezing and coughing that convulsed him so violently he had to grab the doorframe to steady himself.

"You don't look terribly well," the youth helpfully observed. He received a glare as a reply so continued quickly, "There is something important I need to discuss with you, Mr. Gasper."

"So important it couldn't wait until tomorrow?" Gasper responded, having wrestled his lungs under control. "What is it you want with me? And who are you?" he snarled.

"Nathan. Nathan Foxington-Raynor," was the reply. "Sorry, it's late. I was waiting for ages for you to get home."

"Aha!" Gasper cried, the reason for this unsolicited visitor's appearance suddenly making sense to him. A masquerading scrounger! "That's my cat's name, too, funny enough," he sneered. "And my cat wasn't at his relative's funeral today either. Now, out with it! What do you want?"

The youth, clearly perplexed by how to respond to such venom, faltered as he spoke. "Something… something really very small… not even for me."

"In that case, send me the person who does want something—in the morning! Goodnight to you, whoever you are."

Gasper disappeared into his house and the grand old door slammed shut.

Thus repulsed, the youth shook his head sorrowfully, looked the old brass lion in the eye, and spoke these words he had consigned to memory earlier that week:

" *No space of regret can make amends for one life's opportunity misused*"

The door opened again. The congested, inhospitable, scowling head that had decided to wait on the other side of the door until the youth had departed reappeared.

"No *what*?"

"It wasn't for you!" yelped the youth in a panic.

"What did you just say?" Gasper insisted.

"*No space of regret—*"

"Is this for a damned church? Is that it?"

"No! No! That's Dickens... Old Marley says it to —"

"Dickens! Dickens!" The explosion set him coughing again, and he was so long about it, thumping his chest and grasping at the doorframe, that the youth could steel himself to speak first once the seizure had passed.

"I wasn't at the funeral because I hated my uncle. We all did," he said.

Faster than you could slam a door, Gasper's demeanor switched from antipathy to curiosity. He approved of blunt statements. And he certainly approved of *this* blunt statement. "Pardon?" he said, wiping perspiration from his brow.

"We all hated him. I'm glad he's dead."

This was decidedly refreshing.

"You're his…?" he asked.

"Nephew. My mom was his sister."

The two businessmen had never discussed family matters. Perhaps there *had* been a sister. Gasper had no idea. "And you've come here late at night to stand in the rain and remind me of this on the day of his funeral?" he said.

"It's for mom, not me," the youth said, his voice starting to croak. "She's not well…"

"Aha! No insurance then?"

"She's insured. That's not it."

"Well, go on," said Gasper.

"Well, she's become very religious now. It helps her. She's got late stage cancer. So, she asked me to come here… I know it's weird, but she asked me to come here to ask your forgiveness for him."

"Forgiveness?," Gasper repeated, stunned. Not money then!

"It's her religion. She wants everyone to forgive him. He might get into heaven that way, she says. And she gets to clean up the mess he made."

"I see. And you're her religion's unfortunate messenger?"

"She's so sick she can't leave the house. It could be any day now," the youth continued, throwing a sorrowful look at his feet. "I had to come. You saw him every day. You must have a lot to forgive him for."

"We weren't very fond of each other, it's true," admitted Gasper. "Why do you hate him so much?"

"Here," said the youth, tendering a crumpled Polaroid from his pocket.

It was a family gathering, people indoors, posing for the camera. One of them was familiar enough: the huge, angry bulk of Foxington-Raynor standing at the back staring at the wall beside him. On the other side of the group Gasper recognized the youth on his doorstep. Two old folks sat holding hands front left, and beside them, in the center of the photo, seated on a wooden kitchen chair, was a withered looking woman, her transparent skin so tightly wrapped about her skeleton that it was visible in places. She was clearly very sick, and yet she wore a great generous smile on her face. Gasper's eyes flicked back to the bloated face of Foxington-Raynor. In spite of the differences, there was no doubting they were related.

"That's Thanksgiving, last month. The last time I saw him. That's mom in the middle."

"She does look poorly," Gasper said.

"He ruined the day. Just like every year. Even this year, with mom sick. He couldn't stop himself. You can't imagine how he behaved."

Gasper, who had seen some spectacularly offensive behavior from the red-faced man at the back of the photo, intimated that he could well imagine but preferred not to. And family matters had probably been even harder to negotiate with the old swine than the dry goods business.

Whatever it had been, the memory of it started the youth sobbing. The sobs looked very real to Gasper. They shook the youth's frame, they made his eyes water, they made his voice croak and his nose run.

He was a forlorn sight, this scruffy, dripping-wet, soon-to-be orphan on his doorstep. Gasper, in a moment of weakness, surprised himself and took pity on him.

"Will you take a glass of hot port, young man? A quick warmer."

The youth thanked him, gave a sniffle and a sob then passed under the nose of the brass sentry that guarded Anatole Gasper's house.

TOWELS WERE SOON PROVIDED and hot port followed. This latter, unfortunately, did little to suppress Gasper's coughing fits, which continued to increase in frequency and strength.

"I got a chill at the graveside," he said. "The weather was dreadful."

"I hope it's not Covid," said the youth.

"I doubt it. I'm not the social kind."

"Weren't you out socializing tonight?"

"What makes you say that?"

"Only a guess… You left your keys in the front door."

"I did what!" Gasper jumped onto his unsteady feet and charged towards the door, his brain pounding. The youth called after him: "They're in the mailbox—I pushed them in."

And the keys were indeed in the mailbox. A small gesture but one that elicited some trust from Gasper.

"Tell me," he said, returning to the living room and collapsing on the couch, "what did that old pig do at that party?"

"Well, it was Thanksgiving… so before we even sat down mom started on with, 'Let's all be thankful to God for family', 'Let's all be thankful to God for this day', 'Let's all be thankful for the food we're going to eat'—that type of thing. Eventually, the uncle raised his voice and told her he'd paid for the turkey this year like every other year, and that her stupid God had nothing to do with it."

"That sounds like him," Gasper remarked.

"She just smiled and let it go, but I knew she was hurt. We went to the table. I carried out the turkey and set it in front of him. He always carved because he paid for the turkey. So mom said, 'Let's say grace right now and get it done.' I honestly think she was thinking of *him*, trying to get grace out of the way for *him*. 'No grace,' he said, and started carving the bird. Mom didn't flinch but the rest of us did. 'I have to say grace,' she said. 'This is my house and I have to say grace in it.' Then she asked us all to join her, so we bowed our heads, and he said, 'Do what you please, idiots,' and served himself. Mom ignored him. She began, 'For what we are about to receive…' and he threw down the carving knife with a clatter and shouted, 'And you can serve yourselves too, idiots.' He started eating alone, stuffing his face, smacking his lips and making grunting noises, and she started on about the things she was thankful to God for. A minute later, boom! Something in him burst, and he shouted at her with his mouth full of food, 'You stupid cow! You're dying of cancer and you're giving thanks? For what?' That's when she looked at her knees and looked back at him. 'Nathan, will you carve please for us,' she said to me.

And that pig just sat there eating, serving himself more, pouring himself wine, making those disgusting noises. My hands were shaking with rage. I made a mess of carving. 'This is our last Thanksgiving,' I kept thinking, 'and that pig, that goddamned pig—'"

Then he started to sob again, and Gasper felt uncharacteristically touched by what he'd heard.

"Well, the old devil's dead now," he said. "I can easily forgive him for your mother's sake, if you like. Here: I forgive him. I forgive the pig and hope he gets into heaven. Okay?"

The youth wiped his eyes. "Thank you, Mr. Gasper," he said. "The thing is, I know it's a lot, but do you think you could say it to my mom in person?"

Gasper recoiled. "In person? Oh, I'd rather not," he said, looking very sheepish. "Visits are not my thing at all."

It was no lie. He hadn't visited anyone in many long years. Not the sick, not the healthy, and not on holidays or any other days.

"Couldn't you come by just for five minutes? Christmas day, if you're free? It would be huge for her. I could drive you. The house is only fifteen minutes from here in the car."

"Christmas Day?" It had been so many years since he'd had any company on Christmas day. Chez Robert was closed on Christmas Day, and Gasper's own door also always stayed closed. He was almost tempted but answered, "I'm afraid this head cold won't have cleared by then. Perhaps I could call you on Christmas morning… if I'm in better shape."

"Oh, that would be awesome!" sang the youth, suddenly full of hope. "I'm sure you'll be right as rain by then."

"Perfect," said Gasper. He took down the youth's number and stashed it in the pocket of the funeral pants he still wore.

They had their plan then. The ports were finished and Gasper was clearly in need of his bed. Showing the youth to the door, he promised again that he would call on Christmas Morning.

"Tell me," he said at the door, "what was that Dickens thing earlier?"

The youth beamed. "Old Marley says it to Scrooge in *A Christmas Carol*. I've been reading the book to mom in the evenings for the holidays."

"Repeat it now, before you go."

"He says, '*No space of regret can make amends for one life's opportunity misused.*' I would have read right past it but mom stopped me. She asked me to go back and repeat it again and again. 'Think about that!' she insisted. 'Just think about that!'"

Then farewells were said and Gasper, now very poorly indeed, closed his front door on his unexpected visitor. This latter now turned and met the stony gaze of the brass lion.

"Thank you!" he said, with a nod.

The old lion didn't budge a whisker. "Don't mention it!" he replied, in a voice not unlike the youth's.

Stave IV

The First of the Three Dreams

THE TIME WAS FAST APPROACHING MID-NIGHT, when Gasper finally climbed the stairs to his bedroom. The effort required to make this simple ascent seemed wholly disproportionate compared to what had been required twenty-four hours previously. At several moments, he'd stopped, clinging to the bannister, trying to catch his breath.

"I'm truly sick," he wheezed. "Blasted funeral weather."

But he persevered, and attaining his bed at last, he wasted no time in undressing. Still wearing the ill-fitting pants and shirt he had worn to Foxington-Raynor's funeral earlier, he climbed under the covers.

What happened next, no mature inquiry will ever be able to exactly describe, except to say that, as the church bells struck their twelfth chime of the twelfth hour, Gasper had already closed his eyes and, within a few minutes, he was snoring, and snoring with such astounding vigor that no witness—assuming one might be found who could tolerate the noise—would have claimed it was anything other than the artless racket of a man passed-out rattling air through his throat.

Gasper had not long fallen into that restful darkness, however, when the darkness changed to a brilliant, if peculiar, light. He felt he might be waking, and yet, he found himself unable to say if he was dreaming or not.

The church bells had ceased to chime—that much was certain. He had *been* asleep—that too felt sure. But the brilliant orange light that blazed at him so suddenly from his bedroom window on that Christmas Eve 2020—did it ever truly happen?

"What on Earth," Gasper whimpered as he sat up in the blinding bath of light pouring in from the window.

He was still horribly dizzy and felt weaker even than he had before getting into bed, but he labored to rise now, and moved unsteadily across the room to the window.

The light burned so bright, it was at first was too brilliant for him to distinguish its source. But as his eyes adjusted to the radiance, he began to see an outline that slowly and terrifyingly resolved itself into an astonishing apparition. At his window, with a resplendent beam of spectral orange light blasting from the top of its head was a gigantic, brazen-faced turkey so enormous and so fat it was impossible to believe its flabby, clipped wings could be supporting it in the air outside the window.

Gasper stared in wonder at this massive floating turkey. Every part of it—from its feathers and wattles to its comb, snood, dewlap, carbuncle and beard —was colored, not a typical turkey red, but orange like the light emanating from the crown on its head.

An orange-tinted turkey, the size of a grown man, hovering at your window is not a welcome sight! But Gasper was ineluctably drawn to receive it by a blind compulsion he was unable to control in spite of the creature's vile appearance.

He opened the window.

"Welcome to me!" tweeted the orange-tinged monstrosity in a disproportionately tiny voice as it flapped in through the window.

Seeing this over-stuffed beast in all its ghastliness land in the center of his bedroom, Gasper would undoubtedly have smothered it with a blanket from his bed, were he not frozen with terror.

"What… what do you want with me?" Gasper sniveled.

"I am the Ghost of Thanksgivings Past," tweeted the giant bird.

It did appear to have spent many hours in an oven.

"But why have you come to me tonight?"

"For your welfare!" replied the obese beast, lifting a flabby little wing and moving towards him. "I have come to take you on a journey. But to do so, first I must mount you," it cried, and forcing its wing around Gasper's waist, pulled the unwilling Gasper into his grasp where the bird did indeed mount him from behind.

"Help!" wailed Gasper! "I don't want to do this."

"Silence! Fly!" cried the bird digging a claw into Gasper's side. "Run to the window and fly!"

The pain was terrible. Gasper did as he was told and stumbled forwards to the window. The bird stabbed at him repeatedly. He made it to the window.

"Leap!" cried the bird on his back.

"But I can't fly."

"Fear nothing!" tweeted the turkey spurring the hapless Gasper. "In a strong enough wind, even bloated turkeys can fly—and I create my own wind!"

And so, still mounted firmly from behind with a talon in his side, Gasper leapt from his window, hopeful of a rapid fall and death on impact.

Instead, they flew!

Flew into the darkness of the night and away from Brooklyn and New York City across vast open spaces with the turkey's resplendent orange light flaring out, illuminating sky above and land below, until there was a blinding flash too bright for Gasper's eyes, and when he opened them again—

"Good heavens!" he said, bringing up his hands and framing the stunned expression on his face. Here was the town he grew up in! Here was the school yard, and all the boys and girls he'd known as a child playing and calling out to each other, and talking about Thanksgiving and who would be coming to town to celebrate, including the older much admired siblings returning for the first time, the favorite uncles and aunts, nephews and nieces—all were engaged in a good-humored competitiveness as to whose Thanksgiving would be the most satisfying, the most wholly indulgent, and the most heart-warming.

All except one child, a quieter child who stood apart. He had a good heart for playing games but became laconic when talk of family celebrations filled the yard.

"You know him?" asked the turkey, steering Gasper down to take a closer look. "You know this little loner?"

"I know myself, for sure," croaked Gasper.

Then they flew over the town and down into the streets where people were arriving at doors, and thousands of kitchens were steaming and bellowing out fine smells. The turkey stabbed once more. Gasper turned a corner and exclaimed, "This street! This was my street as a boy! And there's the house we lived in!"

"And the day?" asked the Turkey.

"Thanksgiving Day, I think," Gasper replied, his voice suddenly strained.

"Look closer," his mount tweeted close to his ear.

And he looked. And your heart must break at the sight, dear reader, of little Anatole Gasper and his sister June, who will die before her time, in the bare kitchen alone with no turkey, no mashed potatoes or gravy or pumpkin pies but just some eggs and a simple loaf of sliced white bread.

"This egg can be the turkey," says little June in a hushed but excited voice.

"And this one, the potatoes," little Anatole replies, his voice also quiet because their father is asleep on the couch. Where is their mother? A thousand miles away with a new man who will take her out to the dinner and buy her all the things she thinks she deserves—that is where!

"Sad little losers, eh?" whispers the turkey in Gasper's ear, and a tear runs down Gasper's cheek. He wants to reach out and gather these poor children into his arms. He steps forwards—

"Come, come, man!" tweets the turkey. "They are but visions of the past. Surely children and families are *not your thing*!"

And again the turkey stabs a claw into his side, this time to stop his advance.

"Not my thing, no," Gasper echoes in concession, then weeps for a moment with his head on his breast.

"Good!" the turkey squawks. "Very good! Then come take a look at this!"

And in an instant they are flying again, the turkey talons spurring Gasper to fly through the air ever faster in directions he does not recognize until they fly so fast they move though time not space. Here now, one after another, he sees his years gone by. Here is a Thanksgiving dinner of twenty years past, then nineteen, then eighteen and on and on right up to this year's dinner. And in every one of them, in every one–

"What do you see, Gasper?" the turkey probes.

"I see myself."

"You see yourself—?"

"I see myself… alone. "

"Ha! Alone in every one of them!" The turkey is triumphant. "Once a little loser, always a loser, eh?"

"It is so," Gasper concedes, and again tears fall onto his breast.

The sharp claw stabs again. They fly on through time and space, and enter the window of a house he does not know. Here as well, the years roll past, and in each year they stop a moment to look upon the Thanksgiving Feast. And here is another type of sadness, for soon Gasper realizes this is the house of Foxington-Raynor's sister, and there is little Nathan and his sister—he does not know her name—and the mother, determined and happy, and other faces from that photograph he saw earlier, and in the corner, huge, corpulent and mean, there is his ex-associate, Branford Foxington-Raynor, scowling and scolding and preparing to slash open the bird before lashing out without restraint at all around him.

"It was *every* year then?"

"It was," snorts the turkey.

"And still they invited him?"

"These are visions of the past. This is what happened."

Every year, the same! Gasper shakes his head in bewilderment. "I can't help thinking that being alone was not much worse than this," he says.

But the bulbous bird is not listening. "Look! Look now!" it tweets. "Look at this!"

The room is the same. The people are the same. Nathan is a young man now. His sister a young woman. Their mother looks terribly ill. She is in the kitchen, giving instructions, trying to help. A pair of jovial grandparents are propped up in the living room. One is lucid and content. The other lives in a strange dream world and drifts in and out of sleep every few minutes. There are uncles and aunts and all seems happy, and it is therefore a sure thing that Foxington-Raynor has not yet arrived to spoil the day.

"Stop, turkey!" Gasper says. "You need not show me this for I heard about this sorry event tonight already."

"I know you did," the bird replies. "But you did not hear about *my* silent part in it."

And as it speaks, it lets Gasper free of his clutches at last, and flutters forwards into the room where the light begins to increase in strength and heat at the top of his turkey head.

Then a huge shadow passes in front of the window and there is a sound of someone letting themselves into the house without knocking. A chill seems to enter the room and with it, the bulk of Foxington-Raynor appears.

The turkey's light is drawn to him, drawn to Foxington-Raynor's hands and face. He, too, has this orange glow about him, and as he moves from guest to guest, perfunctorily shaking hands, the orange light passes from him to those he has touched.

"What is this turkey? What light are you handing out among the guests here?" Gasper asks. But the turkey appears too busy now to bother with Gasper.

And with the hot turkey off his back, Gasper is again aware of how ill he is feeling. His throat is raw like he has swallowed sandpaper. His head is spinning. His eyes are watering. And his nose... his nose... he is going to—

"ACHOOOOOO!"

He got a tissue out just in time and caught the sneeze. But how strange! Just as he did so, light from the turkey's head came flashing across the room to him and illuminated both the tissue and the hand that held it. Orange light! He rubbed his fingers together; the light spread between them. He touched one hand to another; the light crossed over. Then he put the back of his hand to his nose and there too became stained with the orange light.

The kitchen door opened. Nathan and his sister were helping their mother into the room. The grandparents smiled approvingly. Foxington-Raynor ignored his sister and loomed over his parents, the turkey's orange light glowing warm all about him. Foxington-Raynor straighten his vast frame again. The happy grandparents were now beaming with joy and orange light all over their faces.

Gasper stared at the back of his hand again. This orange light… it had come from his nose. Suddenly, he understood. He cried out, "Turkey! Stop! Stop!"

But the turkey would not stop. It was all a game to him. The light shone brighter still from his orange head as Foxington-Raynor approached his frail and dying sister.

"No!" Gasper cried. But it was too late. The ruddy, blubbery face dropped, the turkey's head sparked, light flashed across the room, Foxington-Raynor's cheek touched his sister's only lightly, but when he drew away, the light remained. The light was on her cheek.

"Turkey! You're spreading Covid to the sick and aged," Gasper wept in helpless submission at the devastation being prepared before him.

The turkey turned to him now with a cruel twinkle in its eye. "No, Gasper. I am spreading nothing. I am the Ghost of Thanksgivings *Past* not Present. All this has already happened, and in thousands of other gatherings of fools, I was present too. It is over. Waste no tears on what has been done. These losers chose to play the Thanksgiving game with me—and they lost."

With a smug and delighted grin, the turkey turned back to survey the room. The dinner was being brought out from the kitchen, Foxington-Raynor was sharpening the carving knife and mumbling how he hoped the bird was better than last year's. Then all were at table and his sister suggested they say grace.

"I love this bit," the turkey tweeted. "Just love it."

Gasper could take no more. The turkey must be stopped. On a chair beside him was an empty cloth shopping bag that one of the guests had brought. He snatched it up and, springing across the room, he leapt onto the turkey's back and pulled the bag down over its head. The turkey roared and flapped its flabby little wings wildly, but Gasper held fast, tightening the bag around its evil throat until at last he felt a weakness overcoming the bird and its struggle became less violent under him.

But, dear reader, we know that not everything that happens in dreams comes true. We know the light of the turkey was not stopped from spreading through Thanksgiving into December and beyond.

This was a dream then—a wishful dream—and in that strange dreamworld strange things must happen. Suddenly, the turkey vanished from the shopping bag and it was Gasper's head in the bag instead struggling to breathe as a desperate, terrifying asphyxiation took hold of him.

Then, in another inexplicable instant, he had left the Foxington-Raynor's Thanksgiving and was home, lying on his back, breathless, wheezing, soaked in sweat and utterly perplexed as to what had just happened to him.

Stave V

The Second the Three Dreams

HIS OWN BED! And no orange turkey in sight! What a relief!

But trying to sit up in the bed he found himself uncomfortably breathless and his body aching from head to foot with high fever.

It was a sorry state of affairs that both his body and imagination had chosen to rebel against him so severely in a single night. If a prescient interviewer had asked him, at that moment, if he was ready for more of the same, we can well imagine how emphatically his response would have been in the negative. Well, dear reader, had you been that interviewer, would you have had the heart to tell him the unavoidable truth—that there was yet much more to come?

And now something else pressing and unwelcome took hold of him: the need to use the bathroom.

"I must first sit up," he thought, and somehow, after a Herculean effort, managed to accomplish this everyday action. He got his legs out of the bed after a similar struggle. There were the black funeral pants he hadn't managed to remove. And there were the church bells again, chiming in the distance, one time, two, three, four… four in the morning then. He gathered himself, took the deepest breath he could manage, which was shallow indeed, and slowly rose.

Perhaps it was a Christmas miracle or perhaps imperturbable destiny, but somehow he made it to the bathroom where, too tired to stand, he dropped the black pants to his ankles and fell down onto the toilet seat to relieve himself.

His head span. He looked sideways to the mirror tiles beside the shower. His noted his skin was considerably bluer than its norm. "Am I cold?" he wondered. "I don't feel cold. I feel hot. And terrible. Just terrible and tired. Very tir—"

And so it was, in that less than ideal position for a man running a high fever, he began to drift off again, and wandering through those early moments of sleep, the first thing he encountered was once again the sound of bells.

"Already?" he begged of himself. "It can't be five already." But bells there were, he was sure of it. Only, these weren't the sonorous and imposing clangs of a steeple bell announcing the unalterable passage of time. These were smaller bells, jovial bells, bells of happier connotations... And then he knew them in a flash—

"Sleigh bells! And today is the twenty-fourth of December!"

This might have stretched the credulity of a man in another situation, but after a far-too-real visitation from a ginormous malicious, disease-spreading turkey only minutes earlier, Gasper found this regular myth of sleigh bells overhead very easy to believe in.

And if proof was needed, here was proof fast arriving, with the sound of sleigh bells getting nearer and a warm red light beginning to glow in his bathroom—a light that seemed to come from across the room behind the mirror tiles until—

More red light, filling the bathroom. Bells and hooves trampling across a roof. Shadows forming now. A voice calling *Ho! Ho! Ho!* And then an almighty crash, the mirror splintering into a thousand pieces and the head of a reindeer with a bright red nose sticking its head into Gasper's bathroom.

"Ho, there! Ho!" called a deep, hearty voice from some way behind. Then a second head poked itself into the room, human this time, and it peered around it at the destruction caused with a huge and delightfully well-intentioned curiosity. "Think we missed the chimney by quite a margin there Rudolph! Ho! Ho! Ho!" he bellowed, slapping the red-nosed battering ram jovially on the rump.

The head was old and wise and kind and warm and covered in thick white hair from head to neck. Quickly it withdrew from the new opening in Gasper's bathroom wall and a huge black boot appeared in its place. Then a red trouser leg attached to the boot appeared. Then an enormous round belly wrapped up in a thick red coat followed. And then, at last, the head reappeared in its rightful place on top of this hale and ample body.

"Ho! You there," the newly arrived boomed. "You on the pot with your pants down, wake up!"

Gasper thought himself awake already. "I am—"

"Pants up!" the booming voice continued. "We're in a hurry. It's the twenty-fourth, you know. I have a busy evening ahead of me."

Here, thankfully, was an affable apparition that a person would willingly oblige, but when Gasper tried to stand he realized he had no strength at all in his legs.

"I'm so sorry," he began in a weak voice. "I'm terribly ill. I don't think I can get up."

"Ho! Ho! Ho! Can't get up, eh? I believe I have here just the thing for that." The new visitor pulled a flask from his great coat pocket and, beaming, handed it to Gasper. "A little drop of this and you'll be fine and dandy."

Gasper opened the flask with a trembling hand and put it to his blue lips.

"Oh!" he said, a second later. "Oh, I say!" Two more sips and he was able to speak with a clear and enthusiastic voice, "Oh, good heavens!"

What was this potion? It was like he was drinking down fresh new life, well-intentioned life, enthusiastic life that was on fire and ready to explore and revitalize every nook and cranny of his ill and aging body. Gasper felt his head clearing, his lungs drawing air with ease again, strength returning to his limbs, and a fire that coursed through every vein in his body bringing heat and vitality with it. He felt restored! Quite restored!

"Good stuff, eh?" said his visitor, winking. "I pinched it from a Wall Street banker's drinks cabinet last Christmas Eve."

"It's marvelous. I can stand again!" exclaimed Gasper.

"Pants up man!" bellowed Santa looking away.

Having obliged, Gasper said, "I'm a little confused. Are you a ghost or are you Santa Claus?"

"I'm the Ghost of the Holiday Present," was the reply, "*and* I'm Santa Claus. Call me Santa. Now let's get moving. Time is short."

Santa moved towards the reindeer whose face was still protruding through the remains of the bathroom wall. Gasper followed with a childlike spring in his step.

"Where are we heading, Santa?" Gasper asked. "The North Pole?"

"Ho! Ho! *No!*" Santa replied. "But you'll see soon enough. Now all aboard! Let's go! Hey ho!"

And so, Gasper's second strange journey that night began. And it began much more agreeably than the first, for now he was sitting beside a jocular old fellow on a magic reindeer-drawn sleigh with silver bells tinkling and warm spirits racing through his veins as they rose high over the magnificent lights of New York City.

"What a beautiful sight!" Gasper cried.

"This much is, at least," Santa replied rather seriously. "But this business we're on won't all be pretty."

"Why not? Where are we going?" asked Gasper, with sudden concern.

Santa sighed. "I didn't want this job, you know, but there's only me and one other fellow who can visit hundreds of thousands of homes in so short a time. You'll meet *him* in time, perhaps."

"I don't understand, Santa," said Gasper.

"You will understand in time, my friend." Then, with a shout of "Down, boys! Down!" to the reindeers, their course changed suddenly, and they dropped from the sky, back towards New York City at a terrifying speed that brought them in low over the tops of the city's sparkling skyscrapers.

Gasper's blood beat wildly in his veins. He wanted to cry out "Wheeeee!" The wind rushed all around him, and he felt a joy he had never known even as a child.

Down further they dropped, to street level now, and hurtled back and forth across the town with a frenzied speed even New York's crazed denizens had never achieved.

Then Santa steered a sharp right down Fifth Avenue, and they roared along for a moment until he pulled back the reins and they came to a sudden stop with a great tinkling of sleigh bells.

"Look!" said Santa.

Gasper looked. There was a crowd. Thousands were gathered, young and old, and everywhere little children with faces full of joy and light, all staring in one direction at one magnificent sight, as tall as a building and sparkling with a thousand lights and glittering baubles arrayed all through its long branches that reached out in every direction as if to touch and bless the people below.

"The Rockefeller Christmas tree!" exclaimed Gasper, his face lit up with fairy lights and joy.

"Yes, indeed," replied Santa. "So often one of my favorite sights, but not this year, I'm afraid." He turned to Gasper and put a hand on his shoulder. "And now, my friend, your true journey must begin."

"How so, Santa?" Gasper asked, but Santa was looking away, staring forwards again over the heads of his reindeers.

"Lights on!" he bellowed, and not one but nine reindeer noses lit up immediately with a brilliant red light that bounced off everything and everyone nearby.

"Oh! Santa! Look at those red lights!" Gasper yelled almost in a swoon. "Look at those fabulous red lights!"

Then every child and every adult close by was lit for a moment in the twin colors of the golden light from the magnificent tree and brilliant red light from the sleigh where Gasper sat.

But the red noses grew brighter and brighter, and soon the golden light from the Christmas tree was receding and all the heads and shoulders nearby because rusty red and scarlet.

"This red light is invisible to them now," Santa said with sadness in his voice. "For now, they see only the homely golden warmth of the holidays. But soon they will see how this other light works."

Gasper remembered the orange light the fat turkey had spread, and a shiver that had nothing to do with his fever ran down his spine.

"Could I have a drop more of that potion you gave me at the house, Santa?" Gasper asked feebly.

"There's no warmth left in that flask now," Santa replied in a sad voice. "But come! We have more to see." He shook the reins, the sleigh bells tinkled, and off they flew once more.

How they gained speed so quickly now can only be explained except by supernatural agency. Up they went, faster and faster, higher and higher, until the world beneath them withdrew so far he could see the Earth's whole expanse beneath them.

"Faster boys! Faster!" Santa cried on the wind, and the reindeers kicked and charged like they were taken by madness and the world streamed by beneath them.

It was too much! Too fast! Gasper buried his head in Santa's great coat, crying in terror, "Make them stop, Santa! Oh, please, make them stop!" But his cries were lost on the howling of the wind.

Then he felt sure the sleigh was falling away from under him, and he imagined it was all over with him. But suddenly the wind stopped howling, the falling ended and a great warm hand came down on his shoulder. He opened his eyes.

To his complete astonishment they were back beneath the Rockefeller Christmas tree.

The street was quiet now, the crowds had all gone home. The brilliant red light of the reindeer noses shone in the night, sparkling now only on the thousands of decorations hanging from the tree.

"Where is everyone, Santa?" Gasper asked, gulping in fear and foreboding.

"They are all at home now," Santa replied. "We have traveled in time only, but most of them have traveled in space to be with their loved ones, alas. It is late on Christmas Eve now. Move closer to the tree and tell me what you see."

Gasper stepped down from the sleigh to approach the tree. The thousand baubles that hung there each reflected the reindeers' brilliant red light from their many facets. So much light and gentle movement, like a thousand galaxies close to hand!

"It's beautiful, Santa!" Gasper called to Santa.

"Look closer!" Santa replied.

Then Gasper moved closer and looked at a single bauble. He saw now that each of the brilliant red facets had many forms within it.

"Closer!" hollered Santa.

Gasper bent closer. These forms in every facet—they were moving pictures!

"Closer! Still closer!"

Now Gasper was as close as he could get. "Oh heavens!" he cried. Each facet was more than a moving picture; it was a home, a party, a gathering of people, of families and friends, around blazing fireplaces and stacks of presents and tables with good vittles and good cheer, all together for the holidays and singing in the new year, and full of hope for better upon better times to come.

"Each bauble must contain thousands upon thousands of worlds," Gasper whispered to himself. How sad he felt suddenly, knowing that these worlds would exist again this year as they had done every year while he had sat at home alone in silence and solitude.

And then another thought came to him, slowly, like when the evening sky fills with deepening hues of orange and red. Upon this tree were hung not one but many thousands of these baubles, each with thousands of gatherings inside it. And every gathering—every one of them—was bathed in the red light that shone so brightly from the reindeers' noses.

Gasper turned away from the tree. Santa sat quite still on his sleigh watching him with a deep sorrow in his eyes.

"I told you I didn't want this job," Santa called, shaking gently his great head. "Now you understand."

"Yes, I understand what you are showing me, Santa," Gasper said with tears welling in his eyes. "Upon this tree are the many thousands who have traveled for the holidays. All will catch this dreadful disease and many will die of it."

Gasper's legs grew weaker under him. Perhaps his own fever was overcoming him, but little he cared, confronted with this forlorn future of so much misery and death.

"Come now!" Santa called over to him. "What is the future we already know? That isn't a future at all! Man is a creature of hope and imagination. This future is very likely, alas, but I can show you nothing that is certain tonight. This is only the future Holidays that *might* be."

"I hope it will be different, Santa," Gasper said, "But I fear man is a creature with too much respect for his imagination and not enough for the facts."

"Perhaps," Santa said. "But this future must fade now, and I must be about my work in the present. It's time we took you home."

One more time, the magic sleigh rose into the air, but this time Gasper shivered all over in the chill night wind and felt no urge to shout with joy. The reindeer noses blazed ahead of him, but there was no warmth or cheer in that light. As they crossed the East River, it seemed the noses grew dimmer and dropped their red light onto the expanse of water beneath so that it took on the color of blood.

Dimmer still the lights grew, and Gasper cried out, "Oh, sad, sad, holidays!" But no one heard his cry. He looked around for solace in companionship, but the kind old gentleman who had sat beside him was gone, vanished into the night air. And now the reindeer lights were fading to nothing and with the extinguishing of their light, they too faded away. He felt himself falling again, this time towards the terrible blood-red water that flowed like the current of time, pulling everything towards a new year of catastrophe and loss because all the merry, loving people in the great Christmas tree could not stay home.

"Would that they were lonely and friendless like me!" he wept.

Then his body hit the cold, blood-colored water. "Santa! Santa!" he cried into the empty night air.

"Help us all! Make it stop! Make it stop!" But Santa was gone, and the water engulfed his body then poured into his mouth and nose and stole the air out from his lungs.

Stave VI

The Last of the Dreams

HE WOKE WHERE HE HAD FALLEN ASLEEP, shivering and breathless, sitting on his toilet seat. By the shower, the mirror tiles were still intact. "A dream," he told himself. "Another sad dream, is all." But he was shaken, more so than from the first dream, because a sense of his own loneliness lingered now in his aching body.

From the skylight on his landing, he saw the first light of the winter's day was arriving. Neither orange nor red, it was the simple gray light of a cold and cloudy start. What time must it be then? Six? Later? He had no idea. He only knew he had to get back to bed, weak as he was.

But standing now seemed an almost impossible task. Just sitting, he was already completely out of breath. "Perhaps I am in real trouble," he thought. "Perhaps I should call for help, call for an ambulance." But the phone was beside his bed. He had no choice. He had to get to the bedroom. And so, in a confusion of chills and aches, of sweats and pains, of coughs and sniffles, of breathlessness and helplessness, he rose, drew up his pants, stumbled across the landing and just made it to his bed where he crashed face down and collapsed immediately into a near coma.

The reader will have guessed by now that a third ghost was coming Gasper's way as he slept. But such a ghost! Surely, even the cleverest among you have not foreseen what was coming next, what was coming up the stairs, step-by-step, unhurried, bringing a shroud of darkness so complete that it chased the very light of morning out of Gasper's house and pulled everything around it into back into night.

One-two, three-four, one-two, three-four went the steps. They reached the top of the stairs. They moved to the landing.

Listen closer! This is not a human step. These are the hooves of a beast approaching! It crosses the landing, unhurried, *one-two, three-four, one-two, three-four*, and now its shadow fills the doorframe of Gasper's bedroom.

Gasper woke with a scream of "Mercy!" and turned to face the dread shadow he feared was come to take his very soul.

It was a donkey! A scragged, dusty, half-dead old beast wobbling on its boney legs. And— strange to behold—it was *blue*!

Upon the bowed back of that blue beast of burden, sat a terrible shadow phantom Gasper had not at first perceived in the gloom. As the donkey stepped forwards, however, he saw this ghoul was also was cloaked in blue, and so scrawny, old and deathly that the donkey looked youthful in comparison.

"Are you the living or dead?" cried Gasper in horror.

The phantom answered not but pointed to the window with its skeletal hand.

"I have seen holidays past and holidays present this night," Gasper whimpered, "and I guess now who you are. You are the death-like figure who will lead me beyond this year's holidays into the new year, mounted on your blue donkey." Then Gasper wept and cried out, "Oh, woe that the old and deathly, and not the young and hopeful with fresh ideas should lead the way into the future!"

Still, the phantom did not speak, but gave a slight nod of its head, like an old man might as he drifts momentarily in and out of slumber.

"Truly then, you are the Ghost of the Coming Year!" Gasper said. "So, lead on! I know not what phantasmagorical journey you have prepared but—"

Before he could finish, however, the blue donkey hobbled across the room and stumbled head first out the window taking with it the grim specter clinging to its back.

Gasper waited for the terrible crash and sound of brittle, old bones breaking, but none came. He staggered to the window. There was the blue donkey with its withered, bent-over mount, trotting off unsteadily down his street, casting darkness all about them.

"Why! They are so obsessed with their own fading dreams that they have forgotten the reason for this dream in the first place," Gasper sighed, looking from the window. "Ho! You there!" he called after them. "Shouldn't I be coming with you?"

At Gasper's cries, the donkey stopped its slow trot, and the phantom did its best to turn its stiff old skeleton back towards the window from which it had just tumbled. A puzzled look passed over its shadowy face like something inexplicable had just appeared to it.

"Phantom!" Gasper shouted. "I know you must loathe this spectral service, but this is *my* dream! Take me with you, please!"

Again, the ghost's head bowed slightly. Gasper understood and jumped from his window.

With no overweight turkey on his back, flying was much easier, and he floated down to the side of the donkey and phantom with ease.

The phantom neither spoke nor moved but stared around him in confusion at the street. It was Gasper who finally got the journey underway:

"Lead on, phantom!" he commanded. "To the future! I am ready!"

The phantom kicked suddenly at the sides of his blue donkey with an impressive viciousness for such an old codger. Then darkness engulfed the street, and they moved forward with Gasper flying at their side.

In the near obscurity, Gasper soon lost his bearings, and it seemed they had traveled a great distance when the donkey slowed gradually to a stop. Gasper found himself in a place so familiar he could recognize it even by its smell.

"We are inside the warehouse of Raynor and Gasper's Dry Goods on Long Island," he exclaimed. "What brings us here, phantom?"

The phantom raised its boney hand and pointed at a group of floor workers who were standing round talking. Gasper brought his feet to the ground and walked forward to stand among the men. He knew all their faces but none flinched as he arrived for they were unaware of his presence.

"Good Christmas?"

"A day of bliss fighting with the in-laws. Makes me glad we never get a real break here."

"Same here."

"And here."

"Any idea what happens now?"

"What happens now is anyone's guess. Two owners in two weeks, you'd almost think this place was cursed."

"Or blessed."

Loud laughter from all the men followed this last remark.

"It'll not be so funny when we lose our jobs."

"Any word on what got Number Two?

"Covid. Asphyxiation. I heard he didn't even try to get to a hospital."

"I know he preferred his lonely life, but that's a bit much."

More laughter.

"Christmas Eve was it?"

"So I heard."

"Special gift from Santa!"

"Stop!"

"I'd sooner Santa gave me a contract."

Laughter again.

"Think we're out of a job then? What happens to the company?"

"They were both bachelors. I suppose their families will sell us off and pocket the cash."

"There's only Number Two's family to worry about. He took ownership of everything the day Number One kicked his clogs."

"Serious? No way!"

"Well, you knew Number Two. Nothing else interests him."

"Has he any family?"

"Not that I know of."

"Or friends?"

"Friends?"

More laughter.

"Well he won't have spread the virus too far, at least."

"That's sort of sad, isn't it?"

"Is it?"

Some laughter and some head shaking, then all dispersed when someone commented on the time and orders awaiting fulfillment.

Gasper had taken a seat on the cold concrete ground of the warehouse. The phantom looked down from his donkey without a word.

"I know, phantom," Gasper sighed. "If this possible future comes true, I will have deserved it. That's all the remembrance I'll get in this world. What more can I expect? It equates well to all the good I've done."

Once again, the decrepit shadow on the dilapidated donkey nodded his head.

Then the donkey stumbled forwards again, first to the left then to the right. The ghost offered no kicks or guidance. Both, it seemed, were on the same senile peregrination with no path in mind.

Then suddenly deep darkness, sent perhaps by the Fates, engulfed this melancholy trio and, on its heels, a chill and terrible wind began to blow.

And this was no natural wind. What natural wind ever screamed and wailed with human voices? What natural wind ever howled the death cries of the wretched and abandoned? It ripped and rushed around them with such sudden violence that Gasper, phantom and donkey were all lifted into the air.

"Can it be so?" Gasper cried over the shrieking wind. "Are these the future dead come to haunt us?"

The phantom made no sound, but its long cloak flapped and rippled in the wind as if it had been woven to give form to this squall of future death that twisted all around them.

Like autumn leaves tormented by a windy day, the buffeting madness threw them left and right and up and down in absolute darkness until, at last, a vast open plain, stretching as far as the eye could see, slowly began to reveal itself beneath them.

Then the sky became the earth, and the earth became the sky, and all about them in the tormented swirl and scream of the haunted night wind, great gray stones like unearthly titanic hail began to crash and splinter in the convulsing sky-ground.

"Tombstones!" Gasper wailed struggling to be heard. "Million of tombstones torn up and thrown thundering back upon the Earth like an endless battering of lost and discarded souls shrieking at the Gates of Revenge against the disregard we showed them in life!"

"Oh, dreadful vision!" Gasper cried. "I know you now, specter. You are the only ghost that travels faster than Santa. You are the ghost that arrives without moving. You are the terrible ghost past which life must parade its wasted souls! Oh, horror, horror unbound!"

The wind howled. The tombstones splintered. Screaming spectral faces loomed and dissolved as fast as forms in gushing water. And steadily it became clear to Gasper that this vision of a New Year weeping in a maelstrom of human loss was the most likely vision of the future.

"In the darkness, I see now," wept Gasper. "For all of us, our work in the old year is done. The lights go out now. No orange or red lights remain to extinguish. It is too late. Here is only death and waiting for more death. We did not take control of the future, so the future has taken control of us. Now, on the cusp of both years, both years are lost!

The tumultuous groan and cry of future lives lost grew louder, and the old blue donkey began to bray and buck in horror. Some deathly fear was upon the senile creature. Gasper called to it through the storm.

"Donkey, I see only a shadow on your back now, a cloak of gloom where once sat the aged specter. Already he has vanished and now his cloak wraps round you with a deathlike grip. Together you led each other too far and for too long. Together you cast darkness on the future, and now, together you must fade. He is gone before you; follow now!"

This poor beast, dead already so many years, refused to go through the agony of dying again. It brayed and bucked until its old blue limbs quivered and began to buckle under it. But the Fates had willed it must die to be reborn in every passing epoch. The shroud of the phantom that had sat upon it for so many years engulfed it completely. One final bray was heard, the donkey vanished, and the formless shadow rag was carried off on the howling wind.

"And am I now abandoned to this future?" Gasper cried to the emptiness.

But no answer came.

Just as he had been so often in life, he was alone again.

He began to wander across the vast plain. The tombstones no longer flew in the air but littered the ground all around him. No more voices screamed and wailed on the wind, but still a biting cold wind blew that chilled him to the bone.

"I dread to walk further among these graves," Gasper sobbed, "and I dread to stay here too."

A slanting rain now joined the wind and together they conspired to lash Gasper from every possible direction. He stumbled on in darkness, through broken tombstones and mounds of sodden mud.

"I have no more sense of direction than the decrepit phantom on the old blue donkey," he cried. "How I wish for a new day, for a light, a guide or even,"—and here he began to weep uncontrollably, seized with a new understanding of his plight—"or even, one single friend in all the world."

He walked on, soaked and shivering, his vision a blur from tears and rain.

"Shelter! I need shelter," he said, and as he spoke, he saw a patch of darkness on the ground before him.

"What unnatural and ghastly sight is preparing to torment me now?" he cried.

But nothing moved and the ground was silent while the rain and the wind continued to batter him in high spirits.

He stepped forward. Now he understood. The patch of darkness—it was no spirit waiting to accost him but the dark opening of an empty grave.

And beside this open grave lay a tombstone, erected for the coming dead perhaps, but blown over by the howling, unnatural wind that had passed.

"There is no name carved on this tombstone," Gasper observed. "Perhaps it has been readied for one of the living we know must come this way.

"And I feel a terrible shiver run through my flesh as I look on it. How the night wind blows and the rain cuts me! I must take shelter. I hardly have the strength to stand. And there is no shelter here except for this empty, unmarked grave. I will drop into it now; I know I must. Yes, cold and darkness are here too, but the wind and rain do not bite so hard. And what is this? It is not rain that falls upon me from above, but soil! I care not, I am so tired. Let the soil fall! Heavier and heavier, let it fall! I lie down, exhausted. The soil comes down and it is harder and harder to breathe. There is less and less air. Harder still my breathing as the soft soil falls and I begin again to sleep."

Stave VII

An Ending

BELLS! CHURCH BELLS RINGING OUT in the distance. The bed was his own, and it was not a grave. Morning light filled his bedroom, and it was colored by the sun. The terrifying dreams had ended... but the suffocating breathlessness in his chest had grown tighter—*much* tighter.

"I must get help," he thought.

He fumbled for his bedside phone, dialed 9-1-1 and found he could not wring even a simple sentence from his lungs. He was too breathless. He must have sounded like a prankster. The phone went dead.

"This is it," he thought. "I'm going to die alone on Christmas Eve, half-dressed in funeral pants, as if I planned it this way.

But these pants! Wasn't the youth's number still in the pocket? Yes—here it was!

Dizzy, gasping, he dialed. It was the youth who answered.

A breathless "Help!" was all Gasper could manage. And it was the last word he spoke that Christmas Eve before he fell unconscious and missed forever the final days of that doomed year, 2020.

WAS FORTUNE LOOKING KINDLY ON GASPER? Had she the foresight to know he would become a better man? That he would wake from his ventilator coma in 2021 and spring to action executing new plans? Reader, you must decide that for yourself. But what we know of the facts is as follows.

Off his ventilator, out of bed, and into life again as the first week of 2021 began, he was already on his way to gaining a first new friend—and family to boot!

Young Nathan's holidays had not been any merrier than Gasper's. Both his aging grandparents had succumbed to the virus that Foxington-Raynor—their son—had brought to them at Thanksgiving. They were old and vulnerable, and simple carelessness killed them. So, they died, but thankfully his mother still lived. Perhaps the virus had died upon her skin. Perhaps she had wiped her face, repelled by her brother's oily touch. Whatever the case, she still lived for now, and all were thankful for it.

And thankful too was Gasper—deeply thankful towards this youth who had guessed the caller right on Christmas Eve and got help to him in time. The grand old door of his house had been knocked in by a single solid boot while the stoic lion stared down, disapproving perhaps, but without saying a word to the people rushing in and out under his whiskered nose. When Gasper returned home in the new year, the door was quite repaired and once again the youth held a key to it in his hand.

"Hang on to it, will you?" Gasper asked. "Just in case… while I recover." And when the youth agreed and said he would make sure to come by once or twice a week for now, Gasper felt a little springtime in his soul.

Much of winter remained, of course. It was January: a time when malicious turkeys were sent back to their roosts, when a sad Santa worked to build a tidal gate around his North Pole home, and when wintry stagnation promised to rule the land for many months to come. But spring will come because it must, and patience is a virtue, after all. Gasper and Nathan saw the winter through, and when the days grew warmer again, they sat on the stoop of Gasper's house one day and spoke.

"I wonder if you'd be interested in another key," Gasper said. "This business of mine—the Dry Goods thing—it needs fresh blood, new energy, new directions. I'm sure we could find you a—"

"I don't even know what dry goods are," Nathan interrupted.

"Ah! Tea, coffee, flour… *dry* stuff, in short. We sell it to stores."

It seemed, however, that working in this sector was not high on Nathan's list of dreams.

"Well, you can think about it," Gasper said. "Now there's another matter—more important—we need to discuss. Whether you're fascinated by dried goods or not, this business used to belong to your uncle and me, and now it belongs to me. And do you know, I haven't a relative in the world, but your uncle did: he had you and your sister.

"So, unless you object, I'm putting it in writing today that the two of you will inherit the entire business to do with what you will when I die. You'll be able to sell the lot and—"

"I do object!" Nathan cried.

"You do?" Gasper was quite crestfallen. He'd been gleefully planning this announcement for several weeks. It had been one of the happiest thoughts of his life.

"You'll say I'm young and dumb, I know, but I'll say this anyway... What about all the people who work for you?"

"Well, I never really thought of that," Gasper said. "We gave them a job, of course."

"And now they can go on working for the company every day, trying to plan their lives, and worrying that as soon as you die, I'll sell off their jobs with the business so I can retire on the cash?"

"Well, yes. I suppose so."

"That's not what I want for the one life I've been given."

And then Anatole Gasper did the wisest thing he'd ever done: he asked the young man what he *did* want to do with the one life he'd been given. And he listened for once without a thought to himself or the old staid dreams he'd built his life upon. And the young man was a revelation! There were other types of business. There were other types of work. It sounded to Gasper like there were other types of people too. People who cared about more than just the bottom line. People who saw a business as part of society and not a path to self-enrichment. People who used businesses to make the world fairer and more secure now and in the future.

"These businesses—these brave new world businesses—they sound marvelous," Gasper said, calculating carefully the enthusiasm in his voice, "Tell me —in what sectors are they appearing?"

"All sectors," Nathan replied.

"All? Surely, not all. Surely, not even—" and Gasper spoke with such deliberate slowness that Nathan, impatient, had to interrupt him.

"Yes," Nathan insisted. "Even dry goods. I'm sure of it. They can be built even there."

"Well," said Gasper. "I'd like to see you prove it."

And so, the gentle trap was sprung, to laughter from them both.

And later that same springtime, Nathan set about his work with the energy and vision of determined youth, while Gasper shared what guidance and wisdom he could along the way. The old *employees* all became *stakeholders* much to their delight, and they now could celebrate how the profits they generated worked for them *and* helped guarantee a better future for the world.

But perhaps no single event of that period produced so much joy as when the young and energetic man driving so much change in the company began to talk of his "*Uncle* Gasper". And this was so much to Gasper's delight that he sometimes shed a tear about it in private and called himself "*silly old goose*" and said "*pull yourself together man!*" and laughed at himself then laughed at what he used to be then shed another tear.

And ever since that day, Gasper had no more intercourse with spirits—or they with him—except the Armagnac he enjoyed at Chez Robert when the occasion called for it, which was frequently because he had become a merry old soul and good cheer for all who knew him. And so it was that Chez Robert flourished, as did Uncle Gasper & Friends Dry Goods Cooperative, and they all, quite naturally enough, lived happily ever after to the end of their days.